DUNCAN & DOLORES

BY BARBARA SAMUELS

Aladdin Paperbacks

First Aladdin Paperbacks edition 1989

Aladdin Paperbacks
An imprint of Simon & Schuster Children's Publishing Division
1230 Avenue of the Americas
New York, NY 10020

Printed in Hong Kong

15 14 13 12 11

Library of Congress Cataloging-in-Publication Data:
Samuels, Barbara. Duncan and Dolores. Summary: Dolores learns
to curb some of her more smothering tendencies and wins the affection of
her new pet cat, Duncan.
[1. Cats—Fiction] I. Title. PZ7.S1925Du 1989 [E] 85-17119
ISBN 0-689-71294-4

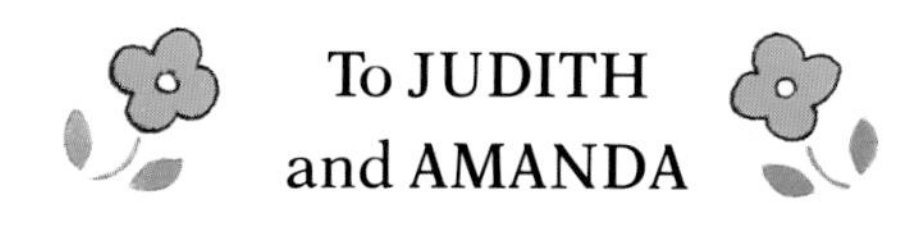

To JUDITH
and AMANDA

One day Faye and Dolores saw a sign:

"He's cute," said Dolores, "and he's just my age. I want a cat like that."

"But animals run away from you, Dolores."

"I want that cat," said Dolores.

"Poor Duncan," sighed Faye.

The Next Day . . .

Duncan was delivered in a case.
"Now you are my cat," said Dolores,
"and you will come out and play with me."

Duncan shot out of the case and disappeared under a cabinet.

"Oh dear, it's starting already," said Faye.

Later That Night...

"Come to bed, Dolores."

"I'm going to sit here till Duncan comes out."

"Just leave some food by the cabinet. He'll come out when he's ready," said Faye.

"Okay, but I'll leave him this note so he'll know where I am."

"Oh, brother," said Faye.

Two Days Later . . .

"I'm so glad you finally came out, Duncan. Now we can play dress up."

"Cats don't play dress up," said Faye.

"Duncan does. Today I will wear a beautiful cape and he can wear this lovely hat."

Duncan didn't want to play dress up.

"I understand, Duncan. You would rather do tricks. I will throw this ball and you will bring it back to me. *Go get it, Duncan!*"

Duncan didn't want to do tricks.

"Here, Duncan," called Faye softly, "you don't have to do tricks." Duncan walked over to Faye and sat in her lap.

The Next Morning . . .

"Duncan doesn't like me," said Dolores.
"He likes you better than me."

"I think he's afraid of you," said Faye.

"Duncan afraid of me, how silly!"

"You're not afraid of me, are you, Duncan?"

"How come you always play with Faye?"

"You never play with me!"

"It isn't fair!"

"It would be a lot quieter around here if you'd leave that poor cat alone," Faye grumbled.

"That's fine with me," said Dolores. "I have better things to do than chase that fat cat."

Dolores made a hiding place with chairs and an old blanket.

Then she had tea with Martha and Mabel.
She did not ask Duncan to join them.

After tea she played the piano
and refused to notice Duncan.

And when she took her nap she hugged her teddy bear, not Duncan.

Later That Day...

NOW, LOOK WHAT YOU'VE DONE!

Duncan rolled the paintbrush toward Dolores. It stopped at her feet.

"Why, thank you, Duncan," said Dolores. Duncan purred softly.

That Night...

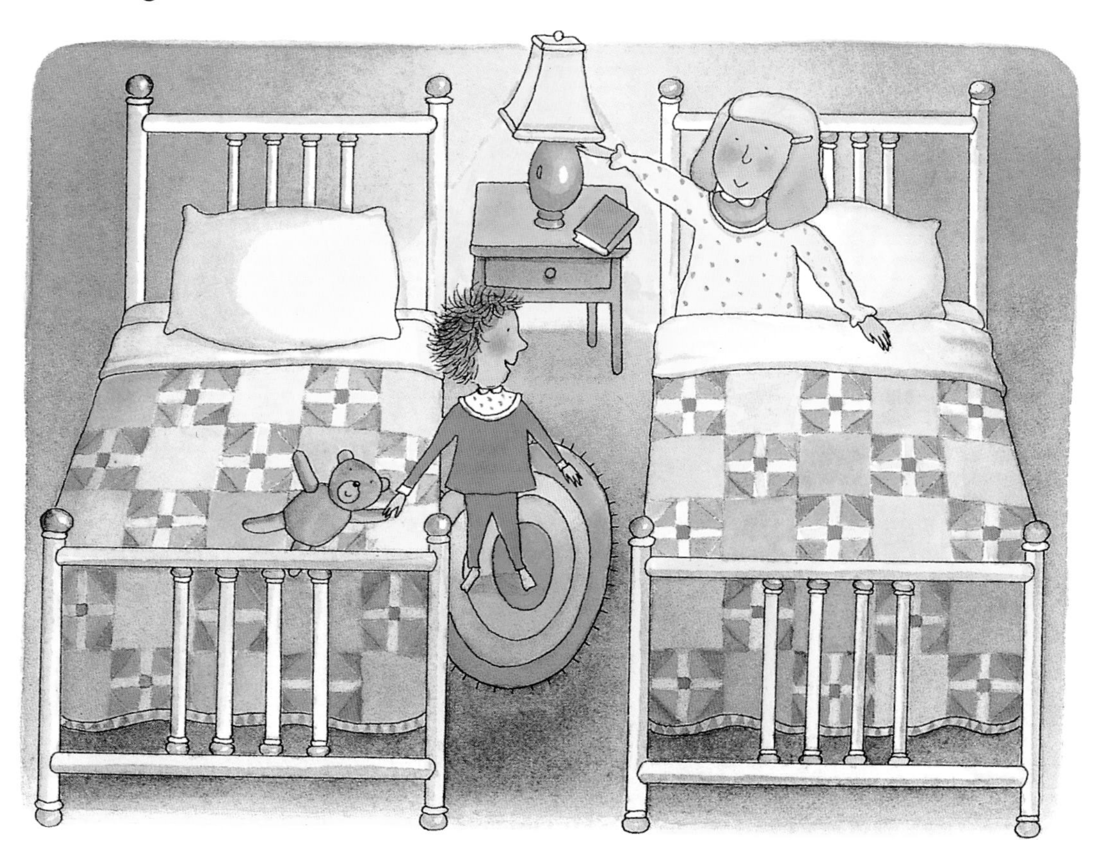

"Duncan sat on my easel today," said Dolores.
"Really," said Faye.

"Then he brought me my paintbrush."
"That's nice," said Faye.

"Look, Faye," whispered Dolores, "look at Duncan. . . .

"His chin is on my neck and it tickles....Faye,"

DUNCAN REALLY

LIKES
ME!

"Uh-oh!"